Woodland Crossings

Books by Stephen Krensky

A Big Day for Scepters
The Dragon Circle
Woodland Crossings

Stephen Krensky

WOODLAND CROSSINGS

Drawings

by Jan Brett Bowler

Atheneum   1978   New York

For my grandparents

Library of Congress Cataloging in Publication Data

Krensky, Stephen.   Woodland crossings.

SUMMARY: Five short fables describe the lives of
woodland plants and animals.
[1. Forest animals—Fiction.   2. Forest plants—
Fiction]   I. Bowler, Jan Brett.   II. Title.
PZ7.W883Wo   [E]   77-21244
ISBN 0-689-30630-X

Copyright © 1977 by Stephen Krensky
All rights reserved
Published simultaneously in Canada by
McClelland & Stewart, Ltd.
Manufactured in the United States of America by
The Book Press, Brattleboro, Vermont
designed by Mary M. Ahern
First Edition

Contents

Clouds

A BLACKBIRD awoke one morning on a breezy day. Yawning lazily, he watched the clouds drift by, noting their different shapes. The largest was especially striking. It reminded him of a bear prowling the countryside for his breakfast.

Such thoughts brought his own hunger to mind. Spreading his wings, the blackbird took flight. He searched the ground for something to eat. Before long, he captured an unsuspecting worm.

"Good morning," said the blackbird. "How kind of you to join me for breakfast."

The worm glanced around for a last look at the flowers, the trees, and the sky.

"Ah," said the blackbird, following the worm's gaze. "I see you've noticed the bear."

"The what?"

"The bear," repeated the blackbird. "The big cloud that looks like a bear."

The worm laughed.

"What's so funny?" asked the blackbird.

"Are you serious?" asked the worm. "About the bear, I mean."

"Yes, why?"

The worm laughed again. "It's ridiculous, that's why."

"Oh, really," said the blackbird smugly.

"How would you know? After all, I have been in the clouds."

"True enough," said the worm.

"So . . ." said the blackbird.

"So what."

"*So what?*" raged the blackbird. "How can you say that? With my experience, I should be the better judge."

The worm shook his head. "Maybe that's your problem," he explained. "You're too close to see the clouds properly."

"Hummph!" snorted the blackbird. "I don't believe it."

"I'll show you how shortsighted you are. Look at the little cloud approaching the big one."

The blackbird looked. "You mean approaching the bear," he said.

"It's not a bear," said the worm patiently. "Anyway, what do you think the little cloud is?"

The blackbird thought it over.

"The bear is bending down," he decided. "Pawing in a stream. He is trying to catch a fish. The little cloud is a fish."

The worm sighed.

"What's the matter now?" asked the blackbird angrily.

"If you put me down, I'll explain. It's too uncomfortable this way."

The blackbird released the worm. "Now hurry up and explain."

The worm stretched happily. "All right," he said. "The big cloud is a cave, not a bear. And the little cloud is a fox, not a fish. The fox is fleeing some dogs. Notice that little dip?"

"The bear's open mouth," said the bird.

"Not exactly," said the worm. "It's the mouth of a cave. Too small for the dogs, but big enough for the fox to enter and hide."

"How can you be so sure?" the blackbird asked.

"It's obvious."

For the first time, the blackbird doubted himself. "A cave . . ." he mused, staring at the two clouds. "And a fox?"

"Precisely."

The blackbird frowned. He still thought the bear was very decidedly pawing a fish. Cocking his head one way, and then another, he tried to imagine them as a cave and a fox. It was no use.

"I was right," he said finally. "Look now. The bear is scooping the fish from the water. He will eat it for breakfast. Just as I

9

will eat you." The blackbird looked to the ground in triumph.

The worm was gone.

And when the blackbird glanced back at the clouds, the fox was entering the cave in safety.

The Meadow's Harvest

IN THE MIDDLE of a sunny meadow, a huge flower grew amidst clusters of daisies, violets, and geraniums. His thick stem was draped with large leaves, and his petals were covered with all the colors of the rainbow. The other flowers felt honored to grow in his presence. In recognition of the huge flower's beauty, he was proclaimed king of the meadow. The new king was very pleased with his position and ruled happily for many years.

One spring, a bitter cold awaited the flowers waking from their winter sleep. Every morning, the king stretched out his petals to capture the warming sunlight. This was his custom, and it had never been questioned. But following the third heavy frost, one of the daisies addressed him.

"Excuse me, Your Majesty," he said, while shivering in the king's shadow.

"Eh? What's that?" muttered the king, who was rarely addressed before noon.

The daisy spoke plainly. "Your Majesty, could you please pull in a petal or two? It's very cold down here."

The king was shocked. "Did I hear you correctly?" he asked. "I should lower a petal for your benefit?"

"Y-yes."

"How dare you make such demands?"

"I meant no harm," said the frightened daisy. "But I need the sunlight, too."

"That's right," chimed in some violets. "So do we."

"What have I here?" the king wondered aloud. "A rebellion?"

"Oh, no," said the daisy anxiously. "But we, your subjects, are awfully cold."

"I suppose you are," sniffed the king. "Your needs, however, must wait until mine are satisfied."

"How long will that be?"

"I cannot say. But your sacrifice is duly noted. You have your king's gratitude."

The daisy could not warm himself with gratitude, but fearing the king's further displeasure, he shivered in silence.

As the summer passed, the intense cold gave way to burning heat. Rain was scarce, and the ground became parched and cracked. During a rare shower, a geranium complained.

"Sire," he whispered hoarsely, "we are very thirsty. If you would only part your petals . . ."

"Impossible!" the king thundered. "One of my petals almost cracked in the last dry spell. That must never happen again. A king must look his best."

The geranium drooped sadly and said nothing.

The smaller flowers were soon too weak to complain. With the coming of fall, they slept earlier than was their custom. The king didn't notice. He was satisfied to have come through the bad year in such fine fashion. Later, he also slept, and the winter snows covered the ground.

The king awoke the next spring feeling greatly refreshed. The rest of the meadow was bare. Cold days and nights passed while the king waited for the other flowers to appear. As summer neared, little green stalks sprouted up around him.

"Ah," he said, "my reign continues."

These new subjects, though, were not pretty or fragrant. The long, lean shoots had only one notable feature—thriving in the bad weather. They soon reached up to the king's petals. He did not think well of this.

"I order you to stop growing," the king told them. "And you must obey me. I rule the flowers in this meadow."

"That may be," replied the long, lean shoots, "but we are weeds, not flowers. And we will grow more."

The weeds were as good as their word. They sprouted higher and higher each day. Soon, the king drooped in their shadow.

"Could you move aside?" he asked the weeds one rainy morning. "I need the water. My petals are wilting."

"Who cares about petals?" they sneered. "You will do better without them."

But the king did not do better, even after the petals were piled in a heap around his stem. By this time, the weeds had stopped talking to him. And the taller they grew, the more tired and frail the king became. With the coming of fall, he slept earlier than was the custom. Weeks later, the weeds also slept, and the winter snows covered the meadow.

The next spring only the weeds awoke.

A Two-Sided Cocoon

A CATERPILLAR rested in a sunlit patch on the trunk of a birch tree. It was a warm, comfortable day, and the caterpillar felt the same—warm and comfortable. When he resumed his upward climb, the caterpillar took his time. He munched on the leaves in his path and continued to stop in every sunlit patch he crossed.

The caterpillar finally stretched out lazily on an overhanging branch. At that moment, a dragonfly landed at his side.

"Good morning," said the dragonfly cheerfully.

The caterpillar yawned.

"What a glorious day," the dragonfly went on. "I've been dancing from flower to flower since dawn."

"Dancing? Since dawn?" The caterpillar shuddered. "Whatever for?"

"Because it's fun, it's exciting, it's—"

"Exhausting," said the caterpillar.

The dragonfly frowned. "Not at all," he said. "I like dancing around flowers more than doing anything else."

"Then I feel sorry for you," said the caterpillar. "Why don't you go back to your flowers? Just listening to such talk tires me out."

"No need to be rude," said the dragonfly.

"At least move to one side," said the caterpillar. "You're blocking the sun."

The dragonfly shifted to the left. "I thought dancing around flowers would interest you. It should, considering what lies ahead."

"As far as I'm concerned, what lies ahead are long, lazy days lying in the sun."

"Of course," agreed the dragonfly, "that's all very well for now. But later, when you become a butterfly . . ."

"A butterfly?" repeated the caterpillar. "What's that?"

The dragonfly looked surprised. "I thought you knew," he said. "You see, I was sitting on a log yesterday when two beavers came by. They were discussing the butterfly season. The older one was telling the younger about how caterpillars turn into butterflies."

"How?"

"I don't know," said the dragonfly. "The beavers didn't say."

Admittedly, the caterpillar was curious. "What do butterflies look like?" he asked.

"Well, they have large wings covered with colored powders."

"Wings, eh?" The caterpillar cringed. "And what do butterflies do?" he asked suspiciously.

"The older beaver said that they flutter about the fields, exploring flowers, trees, streams, and anything else they find. Sounds wonderful, doesn't it?"

The caterpillar winced. "Sounds like a lot of work. I'm not interested."

"I'm not sure you have a choice."

"Look," said the caterpillar, "what you're suggesting is pretty ridiculous. I'm a fuzzy brown lump with legs. Not a wing in

sight, much less large colored ones. And if I don't know about this butterfly business, how can it happen?"

"The beaver seemed to know what he was talking about," the dragonfly maintained.

"Just forget it," advised the caterpillar. "I may not get around much, but I won't believe a stupid story. I have other things on my mind. I'm starting my cocoon today."

"Your what?"

"My cocoon. It will be my first real home."

"I like to keep moving," said the dragonfly.

"Well," said the caterpillar, "my cocoon will serve a useful purpose. Once inside it, I won't have to listen to the foolish tales of dragonflies."

The dragonfly buzzed angrily. "So that's your attitude," he snapped. "I know when I'm not wanted. Good-bye!" He beat his wings in a hasty departure.

"Good riddance," muttered the caterpillar, spinning the first of many silken strands.

Glimmerings in the Rain

O N A W A R M , summer evening, a weasel darted through a marshy thicket into a clearing. He peered into the dusk, cautiously sniffing the night air.

A twig cracked.

The weasel whirled around. "Who's there?" he cried, baring his sharp teeth.

"Just me?"

"Just who?" the weasel demanded.

"A turtle," said a turtle, waddling into view. "Did I startle you? I'm sorry."

"Startle me?" The weasel laughed nervously. "A mere turtle startle the master thief?" He paused. "Well, I do have to be careful."

"Of course," said the turtle. "It's a pleasant night, don't you think?"

"Maybe for you," sulked the weasel. "I've had better. Lately, my cunning has deserted me. Three days without a decent egg. It's embarrassing."

"Never been fond of eggs myself," said the turtle.

"Consider yourself lucky. Eggs are hard to find, not like ferns, for example. If you want a fern, you pick it out of the ground. Period. No trouble and nobody cares. Eggs are different. They don't just grow here and there, and nobody leaves them lying about,

either. I scrounge for my eggs. And someone always objects when I find one."

The turtle nodded. "Perhaps you should develop a taste for ferns," he suggested.

The weasel glared at him. "Ferns wouldn't be the same."

"I suppose not. It was only an idea."

"Go ahead!" snarled the weasel. "Don't stop there. I know what the other animals say. They think I'm horrible. And you'll tell me the same thing."

"I wouldn't say that at all," the turtle maintained.

The weasel paced back and forth. "Well," he said, "I know what you're thinking. The world could get along very nicely without weasels."

"The thought hadn't occurred to me," said the turtle.

"It will," muttered the weasel. "Only a matter of time. But, you know, being a weasel wasn't my idea. It just turned out that way. I've even wished I was something else. Did you ever wish that?"

"No. But, then, I like ferns. What would you rather be?"

"It's hard to decide," the weasel admitted. "I would like a change, though. No skulking or scavenging. Maybe something majestic . . ."

"What sort of majestic?" the turtle asked.

The weasel sighed. "A stag might be right. Imagine me prancing gracefully through the forest." The weasel scampered through the clearing, balancing on his toes as much as possible. "And then to leap over streams . . ." He jumped over a trickle of

water and scrambled up a tree stump. Sniffing into the wind, the weasel proudly tossed his antlers in every direction.

"No doubt about it," said the turtle. "The stag is a fine animal. And he doesn't eat eggs."

The weasel hunched his shoulders and thrust out his snout boldly. "But there is the eagle," he declared. "The king of birds, swooping down from his mountaintop aerie." The weasel dove from the stump, spreading his feet in flight. He landed roughly on his stomach. "Outdistancing the wind," he gasped, regaining his composure. "Brave and resourceful, admired by all."

"Not by rabbits," noted the turtle. "But I see your point. The stag and the eagle are worthy choices."

The weasel suddenly shook his head. He looked up. "Did you feel something?"

The turtle followed the weasel's gaze. "It's going to rain," he said.

The falling drops shattered the majestic images of a moment before. "Oh, well," said the weasel, laughing wickedly. "I must be going—dinner awaits. This weather will suit me tonight. I feel my sharpness returning. One thing about the rain, it soaks us all, the small and great creatures alike. Right, turtle?"

"Not exactly," was the only reply from within a very snug shell.

Autumn Leaving

O N A BRISK autumn day, the wind was howling through the forest. Up in the highest branch of a stately oak, one leaf shivered in the cold.

"A bit chilly this morning," said the leaf. "Makes me feel stiff. And these new colors I'm getting . . . Red and yellow are nice, but I did like the green best. Oh, oh, here comes another blast."

A strong gust whistled through the tree. Suddenly, it plucked the leaf from his branch. "Put me back, wind! Put me back!" he demanded. But the wind refused to listen.

The leaf turned end over end, drifting through the forest. He finally fluttered into an abandoned nest. The battered leaf looked around unhappily. A squirrel was chattering nearby.

"Do you know where I am?" the leaf asked.

"Later-later-later," jabbered the squirrel. "Too busy now."

The leaf was puzzled. "Why are you busy?" he asked.

The squirrel paused in his work. "You must be joking," he said. "Time is growing short. I'm gathering nuts for winter."

"Winter?" the leaf said sharply. The

squirrel's manner angered him. "What is winter?"

"You don't know?" said the squirrel. "Of all the—"

"Now see here, squirrel," the leaf began. He was interrupted by a puff of wind lifting him into the sky.

"What will become of me?" the leaf wailed. "I'm so confused. What is winter? It sounds important. Maybe these birds will know." The leaf called out to a flock of geese approaching from the north. "Please stop," he pleaded. "Please stop and explain."

One goose broke out of formation and glided to his side.

"I'm glad you heard me," said the leaf. "The flock was passing so quickly."

"Well," said the goose, "We're on a tight schedule."

"I was talking to a squirrel on some kind of schedule. Gathering nuts, he told me. He was very rude."

The goose nodded. "Not surprising," he said. "I would expect that from squirrels. They are not too bright. After all, squirrels stay here during the winter." He shuddered at the thought. "I don't know how they manage it. Going south is the only sensible thing to do."

"Uh . . . oh, yes," the leaf replied, wishing to appear as sensible as possible.

The flock, meanwhile, had continued on its way.

"I'm glad to have talked with you," said the goose, "but I'm falling behind." So saying, he streaked away toward his distant companions.

The leaf shook himself wearily. "When

will the wind put me down again?" he wondered.

Almost in answer, the wind dropped him on the low branch of a maple tree. A bear was scratching himself on the trunk. His eyes were shut.

"Hello, bear!" the leaf shouted hoarsely.

The bear raised his head and opened his eyes. "Who's there?" he asked.

"It's me, bear."

The bear stopped scratching and yawned. "Hello, leaf," he said. "I see you're preparing for winter."

"Me?" gasped the astonished leaf. "But I'm not gathering nuts or flying south."

"Gathering nuts? Flying south?" The bear frowned. "I don't understand."

"I met a squirrel gathering nuts for win-

ter and a goose flying south for winter. I'm not doing either."

"Of course not," said the bear. "Why should you?"

"Well, isn't one or the other the right thing to do?"

The bear thought it over.

"Winter is the cold season," he said at last. "And everyone must prepare for it." He yawned again. "But we each get ready in our own way."

"And what is my way?" the leaf asked.

"First, you change color."

"Is that what the red and yellow meant? I had no idea. But why did I blow away from my tree? And why am I so brittle?"

"Those are your final preparations," the bear explained. "All spring and summer you brightened your tree. Now you will help keep the ground warm through the winter."

The leaf fidgeted uneasily. "And then?" he asked.

Before the bear could answer, the wind picked up the leaf once more, whisking him higher than ever above the trees. The leaf looked at the swirls of color in the forest and sighed.

"I am part of all this," he realized. "And I am ready to go where my part leads me."

On those words the wind wandered off to other forests in other lands and the leaf fluttered gently toward the ground.

R

DATE DUE

SEP 5 '84			
OCT 1 2 '84			
APR 1 9 '89			
JUN 0 9 '89			
JUL 0 7 '89			
APR 0 6 '90			
AUG 2 9 '90			
OCT 1 0 '90			
MAY 1 0 '91			
AUG 0 9 '91			
DEC 1 8 '91			
AUG 2 5 '93			
APR 2 7 '94			
JUL 0 1 '94			
GAYLORD			PRINTED IN U.S.A.